# The MAGNIFICENT MAKERS

## MAKERS

### Brain Trouble

Go on more
a-MAZE-ing adventures with

# The
# MAGNIFICENT
# MAKERS

*How to Test a Friendship*

*Brain Trouble*

*Riding Sound Waves*

# The MAGNIFICENT MAKERS

2

## Brain Trouble

by Theanne Griffith
illustrated by Reggie Brown

A STEPPING STONE BOOK™
Random House 🏠 New York

Text copyright © 2020 by Theanne Griffith
Cover art and interior illustrations copyright © 2020 by Reginald Brown

Random House and the colophon are registered trademarks and A Stepping Stone Book and the colophon are trademarks of Penguin Random House LLC.

Visit us on the Web!
rhcbooks.com

Educators and librarians, for a variety of teaching tools, visit us at
RHTeachersLibrarians.com

*Library of Congress Cataloging-in-Publication Data*
Names: Griffith, Theanne, author. | Brown, Reggie, illustrator.
Title: Brain trouble / by Theanne Griffith ;
illustrations by Reggie Brown.
Description: New York : Random House Children's Books, [2020] |
Series: The magnificent makers ; #2 | "A Stepping Stone book." | Audience: Ages 7–10. |
Summary: "Visiting a brain fair is fun, but Violet and her friends get to learn even more amazing facts about the brain when they enter the magical Maker Maze." —Provided by publisher.
Identifiers: LCCN 2019035940 (print) | LCCN 2019035941 (ebook) |
ISBN 978-0-593-12301-0 (trade pbk.) | ISBN 978-0-593-12302-7 (lib. bdg.) |
ISBN 978-0-593-12309-6 (ebook)
Subjects: CYAC: Brain—Fiction. | Cooperativeness—Fiction. |
Science—Fiction. | Makerspaces—Fiction. |
Brothers and sisters—Fiction. | Twins—Fiction.
Classification: LCC PZ7.1.G7527 Br 2020 (print) | LCC PZ7.1.G7527 (ebook)
DDC [Fic]—dc23

Printed in the United States of America
10 9 8 7 6 5 4 3 2 1

First Edition

This book has been officially leveled by using
the F&P Text Level Gradient™ Leveling System.

For Jorge.
I couldn't have asked for
a better teammate.
—T.G.

For my parents, Tony and Sabina.
Thank you for always
encouraging me to draw.
—R.B.

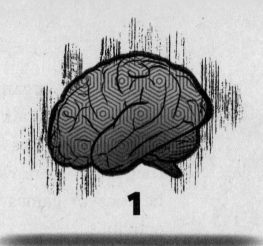

**1**

"**D**o you think there are *real* brains in there?" Violet whispered to her best friend, Pablo.

Pablo shivered. "Gross! Did you turn into a zombie or something?"

"Maybe I did. . . ." Violet raised her hands overhead and pretended to take a bite out of Pablo's shoulder. They laughed as they waited in line with the rest of their class.

It was brain awareness week at Newburg Elementary, and local college

students had organized a brain fair. No one knew exactly what it was—but they heard there would be tons of games and activities.

"I wonder if traveling to space messes with your brain," said Pablo, scratching his cheek. "Since there's no gravity and all."

"Maybe when you're an astronaut, I'll do some experiments and find out!" Violet replied, tapping the tips of her fingers together.

"No way!" Pablo laughed, covering his head with his hands.

Pablo and Violet had been best friends since first grade. They played on the same soccer team after school. And they both loved to order pickle pizza at the New-burg Diner. But what really made them best friends was how much they both loved science. Pablo was going to become an astronaut. Violet was going to run a lab of her own and study different kinds of diseases.

"Okay, students," said Mr. Eng from the front of the line. "It's almost time to go inside."

"Yay!" everyone cheered loudly.

Mr. Eng removed a pencil from his ear and put it in front of his lips. "*Shhhhhh!* We are still in the hallway and need to use our indoor voices."

The class settled down. But there was a buzz of excitement in the air.

Violet was the tallest and tried to peek through the window of the gym door. "All I see are a bunch of fourth and fifth graders who look like they're having fun." She crossed her arms and sighed. "When's it going to be our turn?"

The gym doors opened, and out walked Principal Jenkins.

"Good morning, students!" she said.

"Good morning, Principal Jenkins!" replied the class.

"I hope everyone is ready to learn all about the brain!" She waved the class into the gym with a warm smile.

"Come on, Pablo!" Violet grabbed his hand.

The gym was packed with different stations. At one, kids were making jiggly brain molds out of Jell-O. On the other side of the gym, a fifth grader was making a toy car move using cables attached to his arms. There was also a group of kids watching a cockroach leg dance to the beat of music playing on a cell phone. And at another station, a student wore a cap with a bunch of wires sticking out of it. It looked like they were recording signals from his brain!

"Violet, ¡mira!" said Pablo. He tugged on her shirt. "Look over there!"

Violet's eyes darted to where Pablo was pointing. On the opposite side of the room was a station with five red and silver microscopes lined up on a table. A smile grew on Violet's face. It stretched so wide it nearly touched each ear. Her fingers

started to jitter, and her eyes sparkled with amazement.

"Oooooooh!" Violet squealed. "I wonder if they're looking at brains!" She dashed toward the last open microscope.

But before she reached the station, a fourth grader swooped in and sat down.

"Hey!" Violet frowned. "I was going to sit there!"

"I got here first!" replied the fourth grader.

Violet wanted to cry. "This is so unfair," she said.

Just then Mr. Eng walked up behind Violet and Pablo. "Everything okay here?" he asked.

"I'm never going to be ablc to cure diseases if I don't get to practice using a microscope," said Violet, hanging her head.

"Don't worry. I'm sure you'll stumble across something even more exciting before the brain fair is over." Mr. Eng winked.

Pablo leaned in close to Violet and said, "Maybe *you know who* will send us another riddle today."

Violet lifted her head. The sparkle returned to her eyes.

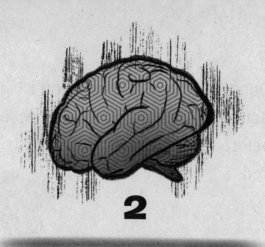

# 2

"**W**hat about that one?" asked Pablo, pointing to a station with a few empty seats.

Violet nodded. "Okay, let's check it out."

The volunteer sitting at the table greeted them as they walked up.

"Hi there! My name is Claire," she said. Claire sat between two other third graders. The twins Skylar and Devin looked exactly alike. Except Skylar had two puffball pigtails on top of her head. Devin's hair was cut short with a lightning bolt

part shaved onto the side. He wore a coral necklace.

"We're baking brains!" said Claire. She pointed to the center of the table. There was a tub of dough, baking sheets, paint, and paintbrushes.

"Ours are already cooked. Now we're painting them!" said Skylar.

Violet squinted. "I thought this was a brain fair, not art class," she said.

Claire laughed. "Scientists use art all

the time! They draw or take pictures of the neat things they discover."

"Yeah, astronauts take all kinds of cool pictures from space!" said Pablo.

"Exactly!" said Claire. She reached for the tub and stuck her hand in. She plopped two blobs of dough on the table.

Pablo sat down. Violet sighed as she took a seat next to him. This would have to do for now.

"Cool!" said Pablo. "What are those?" He pointed to three pointy white objects hanging from Devin's necklace.

"Shark teeth!" replied Devin. "My aunt gave it to me. She got it on a trip to Puerto Rico."

"I'm from Puerto Rico!" said Pablo with excitement in his voice.

Skylar pushed her painted brain toward the center of the table. "Ta-da!" she said.

"Nice job, sis!" said Devin. He gave his sister two high fives and a fist bump.

"It looks almost as good as my drawing!" said Skylar. She opened a small sketch pad that was lying on the table.

"You made two beautiful brains!" said Claire. "Do you want to tell the group about the different parts?"

Skylar took a deep breath. "Okay." First, she pointed to the large upper portion

**CEREBRUM**

that was painted red. "This part is called the *suh-REE-brum*. Did I say that right?"

"Yes, perfect!" said Claire. "The cerebrum is the largest part of the brain. It's really important for learning and memory. And it helps us make decisions."

Then Skylar pointed to a round part toward the bottom that was painted blue. "This is a tough one." She paused.

Her brother helped her out. "That's the *sar-a-BEL-lum!*"

"The cerebellum, oh yeah!" repeated Skylar.

"What does that do?" asked Violet.

**CEREBELLUM**

14

"It helps our body and muscles work together to move," replied Claire with a smile. "It's also important for balance."

"Like when we play soccer!" said Pablo.

"Yup!" said Claire. "You definitely need your cerebellum when you play soccer."

"And this is the brain stem," continued Skylar, pointing to a long skinny part sticking out of the back. It was painted yellow.

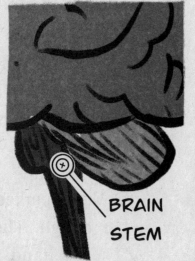

BRAIN STEM

"Our brain stem makes sure that we're always breathing and that our hearts are always beating," Claire explained. "Imagine if you had to remember to do those things!"

Claire showed Violet and Pablo how to shape the dough into a brain. "We need to bake them for about ten minutes. Then you can paint them!" she said.

Violet tried to force a smile, but only one side of her mouth seemed to work. Learning about the parts of the brain was fun, but she really didn't want to paint. She was at a *brain fair*. She wanted to look at real brains!

"Do brains get sick?" Violet asked.

Claire lowered her eyes. "Yes, sometimes. That's why we need more scientists like you! To help figure out how to fix them!"

Violet perked up. She started molding her dough. Then something poked her hand. She noticed the corner of a card sticking out. She wiped it off. It was a riddle from Dr. Crisp, the scientist in charge of the Maker

Maze! She had invited Violet and Pablo to the maze once before. If they could answer this riddle, they would get to go again!

*"Pssst!"* Violet whispered to Pablo. She waved the card under the table. His eyes brightened. They read it together silently.

OUR BRAINS ARE BEAUTIFUL!
THEY'RE LIKE WORKS OF ART.
EACH BRAIN IS DIVIDED INTO
THREE MAIN PARTS.
THE _____
IS IMPORTANT FOR THINKING.
WITHOUT THE _____,
YOUR EYES WOULD STOP BLINKING.
AND IF YOU WANT TO SHOOT A
BASKETBALL OR RUN ABOUT,
YOU'LL NEED YOUR _____
TO HELP YOU OUT!
SOLVE THIS RIDDLE TO ENTER
THE MAKER MAZE.

Violet bit her lip.

In a hushed voice, she said, "The first blank is cerebrum!"

Pablo agreed. "And the last blank is probably cerebellum, since it's important for movement."

"So . . . your brain stem makes you blink?" asked Violet.

Before Pablo could agree, the entire gym began to tremble and shake. The tub of dough splattered everywhere.

BOOM! SNAP! WHIZ! ZAP!

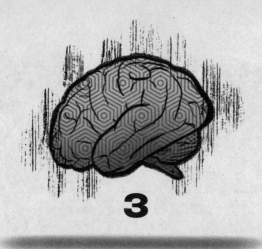

# 3

"**W**hat just happened?" squeaked Skylar.

Violet and Pablo snapped their heads toward the twins.

"I think something is wrong with Claire," said Devin. He waved his hand in front of her face. No response.

"You guys aren't frozen?" Pablo said with raised eyebrows.

"Dr. Crisp must want you to come along!" said Violet. "We're going to have so much fun."

"What's wrong with everyone?" asked Devin.

"It's what happens when the portal opens," replied Violet.

"The *what*?" asked the twins.

"The portal. That's how we get to the Maker Maze," said Pablo, scanning the gym with his eyes.

"The maker *who*?" repeated Skylar and Devin.

"The Maker Maze! It's like a maker-space," said Violet, "but way cooler." She rubbed her hands together. "We get to do *real* science challenges. You're going to love it. Maker's honor!" Violet held her three middle fingers down in the shape of an *M*.

"There it is!" said Pablo suddenly. One of the microscopes was glowing with a bright purple light surrounding it.

Violet turned to Skylar and Devin. "You're coming, right?"

They paused.

"Well, I don't really get where we're going but . . . ," said Skylar.

"It sounds like fun!" finished Devin.

"Let's go!" they said together. Skylar put her sketch pad in her pocket.

They took off running.

"I've never seen anything like this," said Skylar as they reached the shimmering microscope.

"Want to feel something cool?" asked Pablo. "Touch it."

Skylar ran her fingers through the light. *BIZZAP!* She giggled. "It tingles. Do you want to try?" she asked her brother.

Devin nodded and reached out his hand. Suddenly, Skylar's eyes grew wide. "Help!" she cried. Her arm was being sucked through the microscope!

"Hang on, sis!" said Devin, grabbing her other arm.

"Don't worry!" shouted Pablo. "This is how we get there!"

But Devin was too scared to listen. He clung tightly to his sister, and they were both pulled through the microscope. Violet and Pablo jumped in next. After a few seconds of falling, they all tumbled onto the floor of the Maker Maze.

Everything was just how Violet and Pablo remembered. There were lab tables with rows of strange plants and flasks of colorful, bubbling liquid. Creepy bugs with too many legs to count zoomed around in big jars. In the corner, a group of robots measured purple powder onto a scale. And next to a huge microscope was a long hallway lined with doors.

Out of nowhere appeared a tall woman with wild rainbow hair. She wore a white lab coat with bright purple pants and had a golden lab notebook tucked under her arm.

"Welcome, Makers!" she said with a big smile. "You two must be Skylar and Devin."

The twins stood still and stared— a little like zombies.

"This is Dr. Crisp. She runs the place," said Pablo.

Dr. Crisp took a pencil from behind her ear and pointed to the name tag on her lab coat. She took the Maker Manual from under her arm.

"Wow!" said Skylar. She reached out to touch the shiny golden book. *BIZZAP!*

"This glittery gal is going to send us on a science adventure!" said Dr. Crisp. "What would you Makers like to learn about today?" She opened the book to a page with a large question mark on it.

"The brain!" shouted Violet.

"I had a feeling you'd say that." Dr. Crisp winked.

The pages of the Maker Manual started to turn. They flipped so fast they blew Dr. Crisp's rainbow hair every which way. When they finally stopped, the page read:

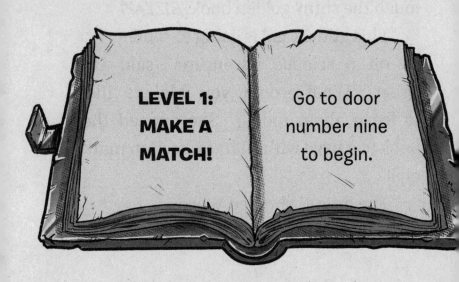

**LEVEL 1: MAKE A MATCH!**

Go to door number nine to begin.

Dr. Crisp snapped the book shut and grabbed a backpack sitting next to a jar of bugs. "Magnificent Maker Watches ready to go?" she asked.

Violet, Pablo, and the twins looked at their wrists.

"Whoa, cool!" said Devin, bringing his watch up to his face.

"We need these to keep track of Maker Minutes," explained Pablo.

"And they shoot lasers!" added Violet.

"Lasers? Awesome!" replied Devin.

"What are Maker Minutes?" asked Skylar.

"We have one hundred twenty Maker Minutes to finish the entire challenge," explained Pablo. He pointed to the screen above them. It showed the brain fair. All the students, volunteers, and teachers were completely still. "After that, everyone unfreezes."

"Yeah, and if we don't finish in time, we can't come back to the maze," said Violet.

"Okay, Makers. Let's hop to it!" Dr. Crisp took off, leaping like a rabbit down the hall.

"Is she always like that?" asked Skylar.

"Always," Violet and Pablo laughed.

The group hurried down the never-ending hallway.

When they reached door number nine, Dr. Crisp shouted, "Let the brain games begin!"

Violet, Pablo, and the twins felt the excitement rise in their chests. Their watches lit up and vibrated as they entered the Maze.

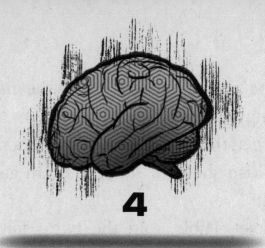

# 4

Violet, Pablo, Skylar, and Devin couldn't believe their eyes. Floating in the middle of the room was a giant brain! It rotated slowly.

Violet's mouth fell open as she moved closer.

"I'd like you all to meet Bob the Brain!" said Dr. Crisp.

"He's so beautiful!" said Skylar. "He looks like he should be in a museum."

"Maybe a *science* museum." Violet laughed.

Suddenly, a rumble echoed through the room.

**BIZZAP!**

The rumbling stopped, and a hologram of the twins appeared. Skylar was painting a picture of her brother. Devin was standing in front of her, spinning a basketball on his finger.

"Whoa!" said Devin, covering his mouth. "How can we be here . . . ?"

"*And* there!" said Skylar.

Pablo smiled. "They're just clones."

"Yeah, the Maker Maze can make a copy of anything!" added Violet.

**BIZZAP!**

A hologram of Violet appeared. She was standing at a lab table, holding two test tubes. One had a blue powder, and the other held a yellow liquid.

"Cool!" said Violet. "I look like a real scientist!"

"You *are* a real scientist!" Dr. Crisp smiled.

**BIZZAP!**

Then a hologram of Pablo popped into view. He was aboard a spaceship, sleeping in a bag attached to the wall.

"I read about those! Astronauts have to sleep in bags like that so they don't float around and bump into things," Pablo explained.

"Okay, Makers! It's time to *make* a

match! Maker Maze, activate the brain matching game!" she shouted into her watch.

**BOOM! SNAP! WHIZ! ZAP!**

A cloud of green smoke burst in the air.

*CRASH!*

When all the smoke cleared, the Makers saw Bob's cerebrum, cerebellum, and brain stem scattered on the floor.

"As you can see," began Dr. Crisp, "the holograms are all doing something different."

The Makers nodded in agreement.

"In each case, a different part of the brain is working extra hard to help them. In this level, you'll have to match the correct part of the brain with the correct hologram," said Dr. Crisp.

"It doesn't look like Pablo's brain is working too hard," said Violet as she nudged her best friend.

"Hey! Space sleep is hard work!" Pablo laughed.

"And sleep is very important for your brain," said Dr. Crisp, tapping her head.

Dr. Crisp cupped her hands around her mouth and yelled, "Ready, set, MATCH!"

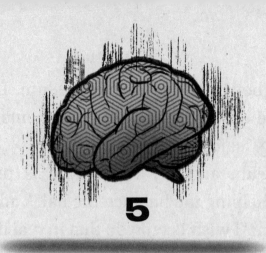

**5**

The Makers studied each hologram carefully. Hologram Skylar's arm lifted and lowered as she painted. Hologram Devin smiled as he gave the ball a swish to keep it spinning. Hologram Violet bit her lip and squinted her eyes through her safety glasses. She examined each test tube carefully. Pablo's hologram snored softly.

"I think I'm using my cerebrum. I must be working on something important," Violet said. "Maybe I'm discovering a cure for the flu!"

"I bet I'm using my cerebellum. Look at the different kinds of movements I'm doing," said Skylar.

"Yeah, and my cerebellum is probably helping me balance the ball," added Devin. "I wish I could do that in real life."

"Which means my brain stem is making sure my body keeps working while I sleep!" said Pablo.

"Okay, now we just have to move the pieces," said Violet.

"How about . . . ," began Skylar.

"We each move our own!" Violet interrupted.

"Well, I was thinking we could work together," said Skylar.

"But we'll finish faster if we divide the work," Violet insisted.

Pablo looked at his watch. "We have plenty of time," he said. "But maybe

Violet's right. If we save time now, we'll have more time to finish the other challenges."

"Well, I think my sister is right," said Devin with his hands on his hips. "We should work as a team."

Violet huffed, and tapped her foot. "Why don't you two work together to move the cerebellum," she replied. "I'll move the cerebrum, and Pablo can move the brain stem."

Devin rubbed the back of his head. "If you say so. But the cerebrum is really big. You might need some help."

"Don't worry," said Violet. She flexed her arm. "I'm tough!"

The twins shrugged and ran over to Bob's cerebellum. It was heavy, but together they were able to push it. Pablo picked up one end of the brain stem and decided to drag it.

Violet ran over to the cerebrum. It *was* big. She walked around, trying to figure out how to pick it up. *Maybe I should ask for help,* she thought. She bit her lip and checked to see what the others were doing. Everyone was busy moving their pieces. Violet decided she could do it alone. She brushed a few loose curls out of her face and got to work.

Violet tried to lift Bob's massive

cerebrum, but it was way too heavy. She grabbed it with both hands and tried pulling it. No luck. She tried pushing it. It scooted a couple of inches, but then Violet needed to take a break.

RING, DING, DONG!

Pablo had lugged the brain stem to the correct spot.

"Excellent! This challenge is off to a STEM-ulating start!" shouted Dr. Crisp.

A few moments later, the twins pushed Bob's cerebellum into place.

**(((((( RING, DING, DONG! )))))))**

"Yes!" they cheered. The twins gave each other two high fives and a fist bump.

Violet dug her heels into the floor and pushed. She still had a way to go before the cerebrum was in place.

"Let us help you," said Pablo.

"I almost got it," grunted Violet.

**ARGH!!**

Pablo pointed to his watch. "We'll be here all day if you try to push this big thing alone."

"Yeah," agreed the twins.

"But I'm so close!" Violet whined.

"Not really," mumbled Skylar.

Violet frowned. *I'll show them,* she thought. She pushed with all her might. But she had no strength left. Bob's cerebrum wouldn't budge.

Violet stomped her feet in frustration. "How come you guys got the lighter pieces?"

Pablo put a hand on his best friend's shoulder. "Come on, Violet. This isn't a competition. Let's finish as a team."

Violet sighed. "Okay."

The twins joined Pablo and Violet as they pushed the cerebrum in front of Violet's hologram.

*RING, DING, DONG!*

Dr. Crisp skipped over to the group. "You rocked that level, Makers!" Dr. Crisp jumped up and played an air guitar.

The twins turned toward Dr. Crisp. "What's next?" they asked, smiling.

Dr. Crisp took the Maker Manual out of her backpack. The pages began turning. When they stopped, the page read:

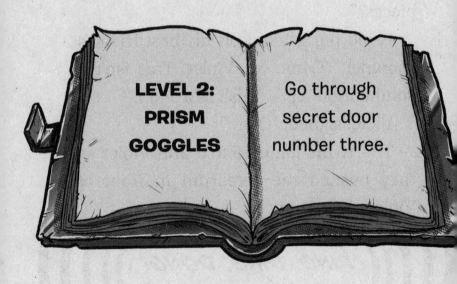

**LEVEL 2: PRISM GOGGLES**

Go through secret door number three.

She closed the golden book and tucked her rainbow hair behind her ears. Then she pressed a button on her watch. Out shot a purple laser! She used it to scan the floor of the room.

"Whoa!" said the twins.

"What's she doing?" whispered Devin.

Violet and Pablo shrugged.

*BEEP, BEEP, BEEP!*

Dr. Crisp stopped in her tracks. "Aha!" she said. She drew an *M* on the floor with the laser. The secret door opened.

Dr. Crisp jumped. "Follow *meeeeee!*" her voice echoed.

The Makers hurried over to the opening in the floor. It was pitch black.

Violet sprang up in the air. *"Wheeee!"* she yelled.

Devin's eyes grew wide. "Is there another way . . . ?" he asked.

"To get to level two?" finished Skylar.

Pablo laughed and jumped. "You get used to the weird things that happen in the Maker Maze!" he said as he fell.

Skylar grabbed Devin's hand, and they leaped into the darkness together.

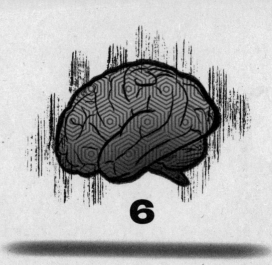

**6**

**PLOP!**

Violet, Pablo, Skylar, and Devin landed in the middle of a beanbag mountain! Violet picked one up and tossed it at Pablo. It hit him in the shoulder.

"Hey! What was that for?" Pablo said with a smile.

"Tag! You're it!" Violet shouted.

Skylar and Devin laughed as everyone started tossing beanbags.

Below, Dr. Crisp stuck two fingers in her mouth and whistled.

"Climb on down, Makers!" She waved them over to the other side of the beanbag mountain.

Then Dr. Crisp said into her watch, "Maker Maze, activate prism goggles!"

## BOOM! SNAP! WHIZ! ZAP!

The room was lit up by a blast of purple light. When it faded, there were four piles of supplies on the floor. Each pile had a pair of scissors, two pieces of bumpy plastic, and safety goggles. The goggles were black with a purple *M* on each side.

"Cool!" said Pablo. He tried them on.

Dr. Crisp opened her eyes wide and cupped her hands around them. "You'll each need to make a pair of prism goggles to complete level two," she said.

"What are prism goggles?" asked Devin.

Dr. Crisp picked up a piece of plastic. "This isn't ordinary plastic. It's a prism!" she said, holding it between her fingers. "These little ridges bend the light that comes into your eyes." She pointed to where she was standing. "It makes something that's here look like it's there." She leaped into the air and landed a few feet to the right.

"So they trick your brain?" asked Pablo.

"Exactly!" replied Dr. Crisp. She gave Pablo a high five.

"We made rainbows with glass prisms

at the art museum last weekend!" said Skylar.

"Yeah! When you shine light through a glass prism," said Devin, "it bends and splits into different colors!" He made an arc over his head with his hands.

Violet didn't have time for all this art talk. She looked at her watch. "Can we start making, please?"

Dr. Crisp reached into her backpack. She pulled out the Maker Manual and opened to a page with a picture of prism goggles and a list of instructions.

"This is pretty simple!" said Violet after reading the directions. "We just stick the plastic prisms onto the safety goggles."

"But we need to make sure the ridges on each prism are facing in the same direction," added Pablo, peering over Violet's shoulder.

"Does it matter which direction?" asked Devin.

Violet checked the Maker Manual. "Nope!"

The Makers cut the plastic prisms so that they fit perfectly onto their goggles. Then they removed the sticky backing and pressed them onto the goggles' lenses.

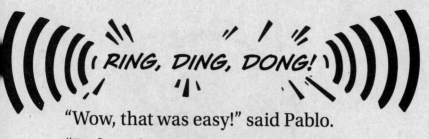

**RING, DING, DONG!**

"Wow, that was easy!" said Pablo.

"Definitely easier than building a boat." Violet winked.

Then Dr. Crisp shouted into her watch. "Maker Maze, activate prism goggles challenge!"

**BOOM! SNAP! WHIZ! ZAP!**

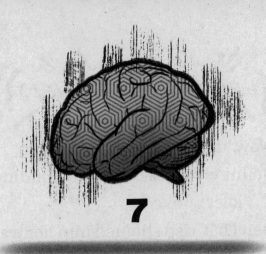

# 7

A breeze blew through the room. As it grew stronger, it started to feel more like a hurricane.

"Watch out!" said Pablo. Beanbags were flying all over the place! Everyone ducked. Except Dr. Crisp! She pulled a net out of her backpack and started catching them like butterflies.

In the middle of the beanbag windstorm, a bright green object began to drop down from the ceiling. The Makers hid their eyes from its blinding glow.

"What is that?" asked Pablo.

Violet peeked through her fingers. "It's a cerebellum!" she shouted.

The green cerebellum came to a halt and floated a few feet above the ground. The wind stopped. Beanbags were scattered everywhere.

Dr. Crisp tossed her net aside and said, "Allow me to introduce you to Sara the Cerebellum!" She walked over to Sara and gave her a pat. *BIZZAP!*

Dr. Crisp looked at her hand. "Fumbling funnels," she mumbled. She was stuck. Her hand was glued to Sara! She groaned, moaned, pulled, and tugged.

"Do you need help, Dr. Crisp?" asked Violet.

"Nope! All under control," Dr. Crisp said. Eventually, she managed to set herself free. "Whew! I forgot how sticky Sara is," she said.

"Now, as I was saying. We learned in level one that the cerebellum is important for movement and coordination. But that's not all! It's important for something else, too. And you'll have to figure out what that is," she said, pointing to the Makers with her pencil.

Dr. Crisp explained the rules. First, the Makers had to toss five beanbags at Sara.

Then they had to put their prism goggles on and toss five more. For the final round, they had to take their goggles off and toss again.

Violet jittered with excitement. She was going to be part of a real experiment! She and the other Makers grabbed a bunch of beanbags. Dr. Crisp blasted a line on the floor with her laser about ten feet away from Sara. The Makers stood behind it.

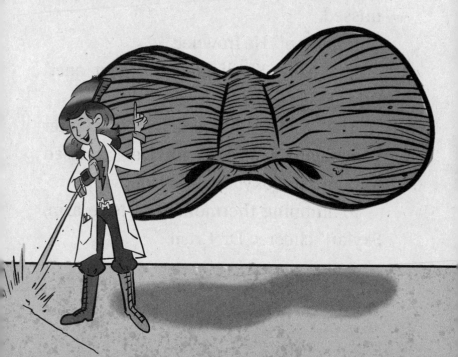

Dr. Crisp pulled a large sign out of her backpack and held it over her head. It read: **ROUND ONE.** "Ready, set, TOSS!"

Violet went first. She missed. "This is hard!" she said.

Pablo went next. His landed smack in the middle of Sara. *BIZZAP!*

"Yes! Made it!" he cheered.

Devin rubbed a shark tooth on his necklace for good luck. He tossed. And missed.

"Oh man!" He frowned.

"It's okay. You'll land the next one!" said Skylar.

The Makers tossed beanbag after beanbag. Violet, Pablo, and Devin missed a couple. But Skylar landed all five!

"Thumping thermometers! Nice arm, Skylar!" cheered Dr. Crisp.

"I think all my painting and drawing helps!" said Skylar.

"Really?" asked Violet.

"Yeah! Just like we learned in level one. It must give my cerebellum an extra workout!" replied Skylar.

"Maybe." Violet shrugged. She thought Skylar had just gotten lucky.

"Time for round two, Makers!" shouted Dr. Crisp, holding a new sign.

The group fastened their prism goggles over their eyes.

"Whoa!" said Pablo. "Everything looks so weird!"

"Yeah, it's all shifted!" said Violet.

The twins tried to give each other high fives. But they missed!

Skylar pulled out her sketch pad. She tried to draw, but the lines were all wobbly. "These goggles are fun!" She laughed.

Violet lined up and tossed her first beanbag. It landed a few feet to the right of Sara.

She tried again. But she kept missing! She stomped her feet and grumbled.

"Don't worry. It's part of the experiment!" Pablo reminded her.

Violet stepped to the side and let the twins have a turn. Devin missed his first couple of throws, too. The same happened for Skylar and Pablo.

Violet bit her lip. She noticed the beanbags kept landing to the right. She decided to try changing how she tossed them.

***BIZZAP!***

"I did it!" Violet said proudly.

After making some adjustments, Pablo and the twins eventually landed beanbags on Sara, too.

"Time for round three! Goggles off!" Dr. Crisp shouted as she jogged around holding the final sign.

Violet stepped up to toss. "This should

be easy!" she said. Everything looked normal again. But she missed! So did Pablo and the twins.

"I wonder why we can't land them," Pablo said. Everyone had tossed a few more times with no luck.

"Let me try something," said Skylar, stepping up to the line.

She paused for a few seconds before throwing her beanbag very carefully.
**BIZZAP!**

"Bumbling beakers!" said Dr. Crisp. "You did it!"

"You guys, I have an idea!" said Skylar.

Violet ignored Skylar and went to grab some more beanbags.

"I want to try again," she said.

"But Skylar has an idea," said Devin.

"I think I know what else the cerebellum does!" said Skylar. "When I—"

"Just hold on a sec!" interrupted Violet. She stood very still and tossed. She missed. She tried again. And she missed again. And again.

"Argh!" she yelled. She ran toward Sara and jumped with her leg stretched out in a karate kick. As Violet flew through the air, she suddenly felt a sinking feeling in her stomach.

BIZZAP!

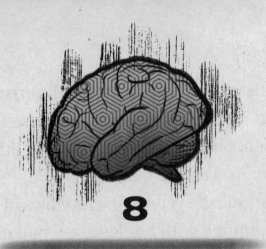

# 8

"¡Ay, Dios! Violet, look what you did!" said Pablo.

Skylar and Devin gasped.

Violet was stuck. And she was hanging upside down! Her right foot and leg were glued to the middle of Sara the Cerebellum. She tried to kick herself loose with her left leg. But it was no use. That leg got stuck, too. Her fingertips swayed above the floor as she squirmed and wiggled.

"Get me down! Get me down!" Violet begged.

"Now, *this* is a sticky situation," said Dr. Crisp, rubbing her chin.

Pablo ran over to help Violet. As he tried to pull her off, his hand became glued to Sara as well.

"¡Caramba!" he said.

Skylar and Devin hurried over to help. But before they knew it, all four Makers were stuck to Sara.

"What are we going to do?" cried Violet.

"This challenge wasn't about being the best beanbag thrower!" Devin said through clenched teeth.

"It was about working as a *team* to solve a problem," added Skylar.

"At least *now* you all are sticking together!" joked Dr. Crisp.

No one laughed.

Violet lowered her eyes. "I know I let everyone down. I was just so excited about this challenge."

"It's okay, Violet. We all make mistakes and get carried away sometimes," said Pablo. "You're just passionate."

But the twins stared down at Violet with cold faces.

After a few moments of silence, Violet said, "I'm really sorry. I mean it. I made this level more about me than working together." She tried to twist her body toward Skylar. "And I'm sorry I didn't listen to you when I should have. I just didn't want you to be the one to guess the answer."

Skylar raised her eyebrows. "But why?"

Violet paused. "Because you're into art. I didn't want to lose to someone who doesn't even like science."

"We do like science!" replied Devin.

Then Skylar's face softened. "But maybe not as much as you," she said with a smile. "I understand what it feels like to want to be the best at something you love. I was so sad when I came in second place in the art show last year."

Violet gave Skylar an upside-down smile. "Let's get ourselves unstuck. As a team!"

Pablo looked at his Magnificent Maker Watch. "We're going to run out of time if we don't hurry!"

"Sis, what were you going to say?" asked Devin.

"Yeah, Skylar, tell us your idea!" said Violet.

"Well, at first it was pretty easy to land the beanbags," Skylar said. "But with the goggles on, we started missing."

"We got better, though," added Devin.

"We did! We *learned*! Then, when we took the goggles off, we started missing again," Skylar continued.

Violet bit her lip. "It's like we had to *relearn* how to throw with normal vision."

"So that means . . . ," Pablo began.

"Our cerebellums also must be important for *learning* how to move!" shouted Skylar.

RING, DING, DONG!

Sara lost her stickiness. Pablo and the twins freed themselves. Violet crashed to the floor.

"Way to *stick* that one out and finish strong!" cheered Dr. Crisp.

"Will my cerebellum help me learn to move in zero gravity when I become

an astronaut?" asked Pablo as he helped Violet up.

Dr. Crisp thought for a moment and said, "I'm not sure! But that sounds like an experiment that you and Violet could work on together. As a team." She winked.

"You guys, we only have thirty Maker Minutes left!" shouted Devin as he held up his watch.

"Hopping hot plates! We should get a move on!"

68

said Dr. Crisp. She pulled the Maker Manual out of her backpack, and it snapped open.

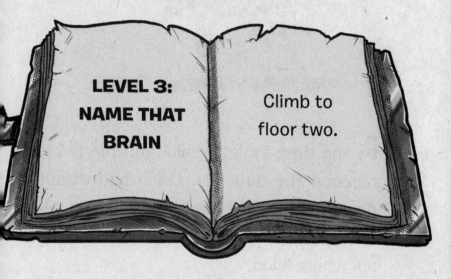

LEVEL 3:
NAME THAT
BRAIN

Climb to
floor two.

Dr. Crisp threw the book in her backpack and took off running toward a door in the corner of the room. She opened it and yelled back to the Makers, "Follow me!"

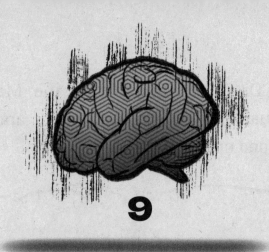

## 9

By the time Violet, Pablo, and the twins reached the door, Dr. Crisp had disappeared. Inside the small room was a tall red ladder. They looked up but couldn't tell where it led.

"Wait, we actually have to climb?" asked Devin, rubbing the back of his head.

"You'd think with all the lasers and holograms, the Maker Maze would at least have an elevator," said Skylar.

"Exercise is good for your brain!"

echoed a voice from above. It was Dr. Crisp!

Everyone laughed. One by one they started climbing. After what felt like a very long time, the Makers made it to the top. The tip of the ladder rested on the edge of the opening in the floor. Violet, Pablo, and the twins pulled themselves up and wiped the sweat off their foreheads.

"Welcome to level three!" said Dr. Crisp.

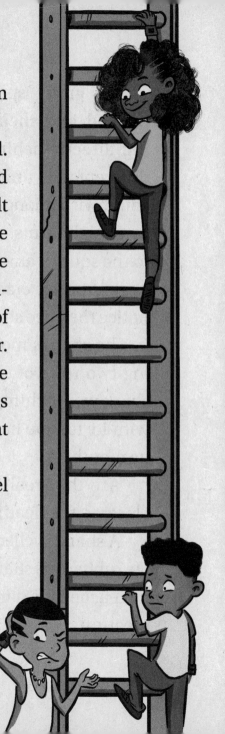

The group spun around. Their eyes popped and their jaws dropped. Floating directly behind Dr. Crisp were four different wild animals! There was a giant squid with a long pink head, two glaring eyes, eight arms, and two tentacles. Next to the squid was a rat. It was nibbling on a peanut butter cracker and didn't seem to notice the huge shark floating right next to it. The shark's mouth hung open, revealing two rows of sharp teeth. Next to the shark was a chimpanzee. It was smiling, with its tongue hanging out of the side of its mouth.

"Are they real?" asked Violet, inching closer to the floating animals.

"A shark!" yelled Devin. "I love sharks!" He rubbed his shark-tooth necklace. Then he reached his hand toward the fierce sea creature.

**CHOMP!**

The shark slammed its jaws shut!

"Be careful!" Skylar cried.

Dr. Crisp walked over and waved her hand through the beast. **BIZZAP!** "They're just holograms!"

Pablo scratched his cheek. "I thought we were learning about brains."

Dr. Crisp smiled and said into her watch, "Maker Maze, activate *name that brain*!"

The floor started to shake. The animals were trembling, too!

**BOOM! SNAP! WHIZ! ZAP!**

Four floating brains appeared on the opposite side of the room.

"No way!" said Violet. She ran over and

stopped right in front of them. She reached out to touch one.

**BIZZAP!**

Violet giggled. Pablo and the twins joined her. They walked in a circle around the brains. Each one looked different. One was small and smooth. Another was large and bumpy. The next brain looked like a donut. And the last one looked like it had antennas coming out of the top.

"That one has to be an alien brain!" said Pablo, pointing to the one with the antennas.

"No aliens here! Just animals. Now, listen up, Makers!" said Dr. Crisp, clapping as she walked to the center of the room. "In the first two levels, you learned about different parts of the brain. But not all brains look the same!"

With one hand, she pointed to the brains, and with the other, she pointed to the animals. "To complete this level and finish the challenge, you will have to decide which brain belongs to which animal. You'll use your Magnificent Maker Watches to scan the brain and then scan the correct animal," said Dr. Crisp. She pointed to a button on their watches.

"Yes! We finally get to shoot lasers!" said Devin.

Then Dr. Crisp gave them one more piece of advice. "If you get stuck, think about what makes each animal special. What makes an animal special also makes their brain special."

Dr. Crisp crossed her arms so that her fingers were pointing in opposite directions. "Ready, set, SCAN!"

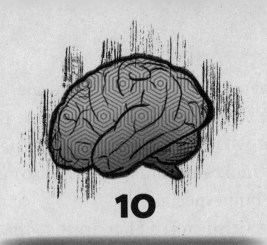

# 10

"Let's start with the easiest one first," said Violet, pointing to the small brain. "That one has to belong to the rat."

Everyone agreed.

"Do you want to scan it?" she asked Devin.

"Sure!" he said. He pointed his watch at the brain. A purple laser shot out.

"AWESOME!" he said. Devin walked over to the rat.

*CHOMP!*

"That's one sassy shark!" Dr. Crisp laughed.

Devin crept a little closer. He scanned the rat, and a check mark appeared on his watch.

**RING, DING, DONG!**

"Yeah!" everyone shouted. They all gave each other high fives.

"That's how you Maker Match!" cheered Dr. Crisp.

"What about that one?" asked Pablo, pointing to the bigger, bumpy brain.

"I bet it belongs to the chimp!" said Skylar. "It looks like a human brain. And humans and chimpanzees are kind of like cousins in the animal world!"

Skylar scanned the brain and then the chimpanzee.

**RING, DING, DONG!**

"Okay, we have two left," said Violet. She rubbed her chin. "A donut brain and a . . ." She paused.

"An alien brain!" finished Pablo.

Everyone laughed. They studied the brains carefully.

"We have to think like scientists," said Violet. "Remember what Dr. Crisp said? What's special about sharks?"

"No idea," replied Pablo.

"Sharks are really good hunters!" Devin

said. "I watched this documentary during shark week. Did you know they can smell blood . . . ?"

"That's it!" Skylar yelled.

"What's it?" asked Violet.

"Before you guys sat down with us at the brain fair, Claire was talking about bulbs in our brain," she continued.

"Like lightbulbs?" asked Pablo.

Skylar was talking so fast she could

barely catch her breath. "No. They were for smelling. She said we have small ones. But they can be pretty big in some animals! Especially animals with a good sense of smell!"

Dr. Crisp pulled a rose out of her lab coat and sniffed it. "They're called *ol-FAC-to-ry* bulbs."

"So you think the antennas on the alien brain are olfactory bulbs?" asked Violet.

"Maybe?" Skylar replied.

"I see some *bulbs* lighting up in those Maker minds!" cheered Dr. Crisp.

"If sharks have a really good sense of smell, then maybe the alien brain is actually a shark brain!" said Pablo.

"Give it a try!" said Violet.

Pablo aimed his watch and scanned the alien brain and then the shark.

## RING, DING, DONG!

Violet, Pablo, and the twins jumped up and down with excitement.

"The donut brain must belong to the squid then," said Violet. She aimed and scanned.

## RING, DING, DONG!

"Tumbling test tubes! That's what I call *teamwork*!" said Dr. Crisp. She gave each Maker a double high five.

Violet turned to Dr. Crisp and asked, "Why is the squid brain shaped like a donut?"

"The squid's brain is in the middle of its body!" Dr. Crisp made an O shape with her hand. "Food has to go through the brain to get from its mouth to its stomach," she explained.

"That's pretty weird," said Pablo. "Maybe squid are alien spies!"

Suddenly, Dr. Crisp's watch started flashing purple.

"We only have three Maker Minutes before the portal closes!" shouted Violet.

"That way!" said Dr. Crisp, pointing to a door on the opposite end of the room.

When they opened it, they realized they were at door number twenty-two!

"How did we get *here*?" asked Skylar.

Dr. Crisp bolted down the long hallway.

"Run!" yelled Violet.

After a long sprint, the Makers finally

arrived in the main lab of the Maker Maze. They were completely out of breath.

Dr. Crisp pointed to the portal on the ceiling. She knocked over a beaker that was sitting on a lab table. Dark liquid spilled everywhere.

Dr. Crisp didn't seem to notice. "Just jump!" she said.

Pablo and Devin ran over and jumped as high as they could.

## BOOM! SNAP! WHIZ! ZAP!

Skylar tried next. But she was so tired from running she couldn't jump high enough.

"Hurry, get on my shoulders!" said Violet.

Violet bent down so Skylar could climb  up. She stood up on shaky knees.

"Thirty seconds!" Dr. Crisp yelled.

"Hold on tight!" Violet hollered to Skylar. "One, two, THREE!"

Violet jumped with all

her might as Skylar reached for the portal. Skylar's fingertips got just close enough for both of them to be sucked in.

**BOOM! SNAP! WHIZ! ZAP!**

They rolled onto the floor of the gym, crashing into Pablo and Devin.

"Hurry! Everyone is still frozen!" said Pablo.

Just as they sat down, everyone unfroze. The brain fair sprang to life again.

Claire began talking. "This is my first time volunteering at a brain fair. I'm having so much fun!" Then she wiped her cheek. "Is this dough?" she asked.

It had flown everywhere when the portal opened.

"Sorry," the Makers said.

"It's okay! Science gets messy some-times." Claire laughed.

Then Mr. Eng walked toward them.

"Hey, Violet, there are a few free seats at the microscope station," he said, and pointed with his pencil.

"Oh, thanks, Mr. Eng! I'll go check it out." Violet smiled.

Mr. Eng's shoes squeaked as he walked away.

"Are his shoes wet?" Pablo whispered to Violet.

She shrugged. Then Violet turned to Claire. "Did you know squids have donuts for brains?"

# Make your own creations!

## ⇒MAKE PRISM GOGGLES!⇐

Always *make* carefully and with adult supervision!

## MATERIALS

1 pair of plastic safety goggles with flat frames

2 press-on Fresnel prisms (30 diopter)*

5 beanbags
    masking tape or chalk
    plastic bucket
    scissors

*These can be purchased at your local medical supply store or online.

90

## INSTRUCTIONS

1. Examine each Fresnel prism carefully. Note which direction the ridges are pointing. For step two, they should be pointing in the same direction.

2. Lay one prism over one goggle lens. Use scissors to carefully cut the prism so it fits exactly over the lens. Repeat for the other lens using the second prism.

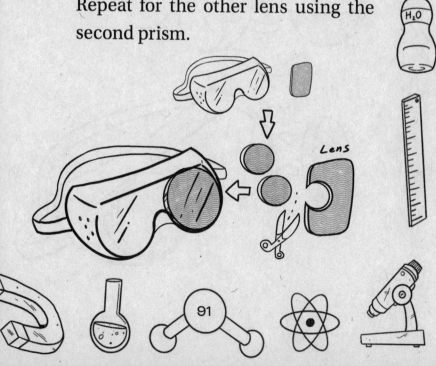

Lens

3. Make sure the goggles' lenses are clean and dry.

4. Remove the backing from the Fresnel prism to expose the sticky side. Press it firmly onto one of the lenses, making sure not to create any air pockets. Repeat for the other prism.

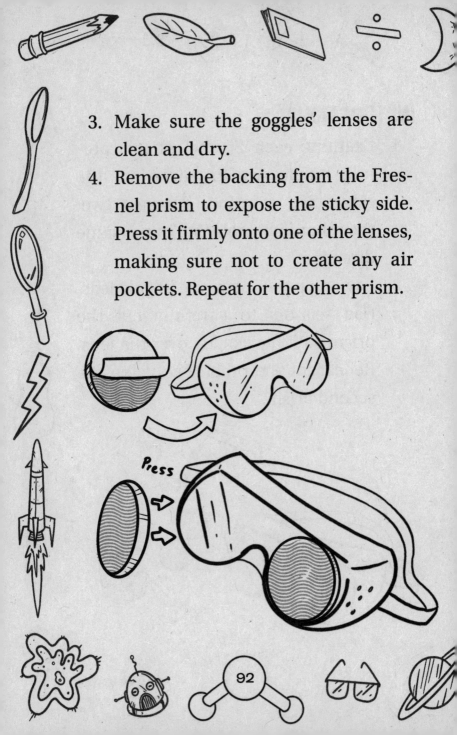

Press

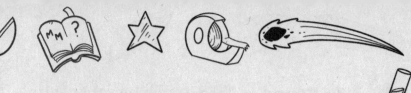

## HOW TO PLAY THE PRISM GOGGLES CHALLENGE

1. Find a safe, open space inside or outside. Mark a line with masking tape (inside) or chalk (outside). This is where you will stand to toss the beanbags. Place the plastic bucket five to ten feet in front of your line.

5-10 FEET

BEAN BAGS

2. **Round 1:** Throw each beanbag, aiming for the bucket. Record how many beanbags landed in the bucket.* (You can throw as many times as you want! Just make sure to throw an equal number of beanbags in each round.)

3. **Round 2:** Put on your prism goggles. Try to land the beanbags in the bucket. What happened? Record how many beanbags landed in the bucket and note any observations.

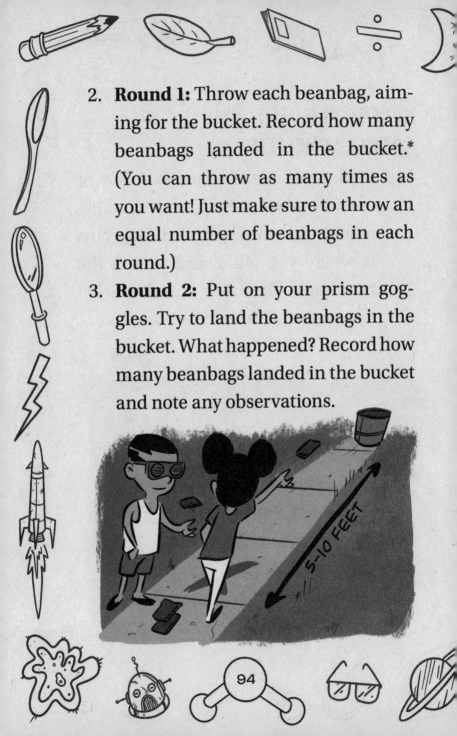

5–10 FEET

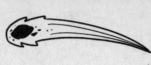

4. **Round 3:** Take off your prism goggles and toss again. What is different from round 2? Record how many beanbags landed in the bucket and note any observations.

*You can create your own experiment sheet or download one at theannegriffith.com.

Your parent or guardian can share pictures and videos of your prism goggles challenge on social media using #MagnificentMakers.

# ⋛BAKE A BRAIN!⋜

## MATERIALS

- ¼ cup salt
- ⅓ to ½ cup water
- 1 cup flour, plus 1 tablespoon
- baking sheet
- large bowl
- oven
- paint
- paintbrushes (or your fingers!)
- large spoon for stirring

## INSTRUCTIONS

1. Mix the salt and flour in a large bowl.
2. Slowly add water until the dough is no longer crumbly.
3. Sprinkle 1 tablespoon of flour on the countertop or on a cutting board.

4. Form the dough into a ball and knead until it can be molded easily.
5. Shape the dough into a brain! Use the outline provided as a guide.

6. Place the brain on an ungreased baking sheet and bake for 10–15 minutes at 350°F.*

*Ask an adult for help!

7. Allow your brain to cool, and then paint it! You can make it all one color or paint each part of the brain different colors. Get creative!

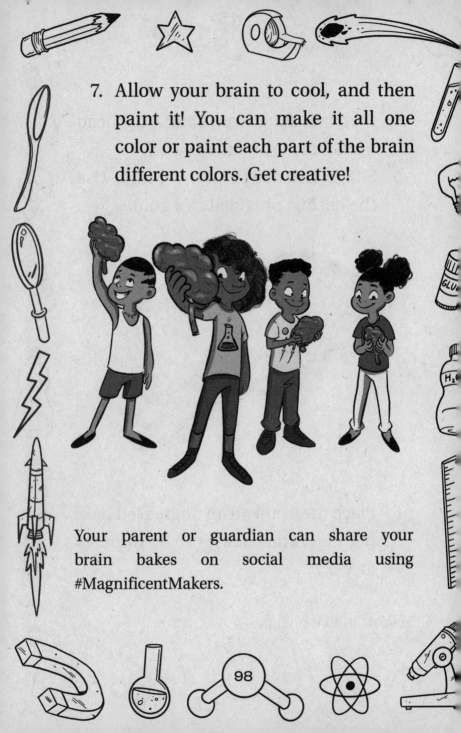

Your parent or guardian can share your brain bakes on social media using #MagnificentMakers.

# Missing the
# **Maker Maze** already?

## Read on for a peek at the
## Magnificent Makers' next adventure!

The room was pitch-black. All the Makers could hear was the sound of one another's breathing. Suddenly, Dr. Crisp's voice boomed over a loudspeaker.

"Step right up, step right up, Makers! Welcome to the first level of your sensory adventure!"

Henry frowned as he covered his ears.

The lights flashed on, and the room glowed purple. Wide streamers and banners draped the ceiling. Colorful, confetti-filled balloons floated through the air. They were tied into different animal shapes. At the far end of the room, Dr. Crisp stood on a stage in the middle of a spotlight. Next to her was a large black box with a purple *M* painted on the side.

"This is a circus," said Henry, pulling on his sleeve. "Not a makerspace." A giant llama balloon floated over his head. "I don't know if I like it."

"Don't worry, I'm sure you're going to love it!" said Violet with a smile. She darted toward the stage. Pablo and Henry hurried after her.

"In this level, we are going to explore our sense of touch," said Dr. Crisp, tapping her pointer fingers together. "And we'll be using this Mystery Maker Box!" She gave the box a slap.

"How does it work?" Pablo asked.

"This box is full of all kinds of goodies," Dr. Crisp began.

"Like candy?" asked Henry.

"Not this time." Dr. Crisp laughed. Then she pointed to a hole in the top of the box. "In the first part of the level, you'll stick your hands in here and dig around. When you grab something, you'll have to guess what it is. But you can *only* use your hands. No peeking! And you have to guess correctly before you take the item out of the box."

Dr. Crisp opened her backpack. "Here are your Mystery Mittens!" she said, tossing each Maker a pair. "In the second part, you're going to guess what you grab while wearing these. You might notice . . . a difference." Dr. Crisp winked. "To complete the level, you'll have to figure out why it's so different exploring the Mystery Maker Box with mittens on."

"There isn't anything in there that can

hurt us, right?" asked Henry, peering through the dark opening.

"Most definitely not!" replied Dr. Crisp. She held up her right hand with her three middle fingers down, making an *M*. "Maker's honor." Then she pressed a button on the side of her watch. "Activate Mystery Maker Box!" The watch glowed purple. "Ready, set, DIG!"

# Acknowledgments

Thank you, Jorge, for your unwavering encouragement. Dad, I am forever grateful that you instilled in me a love for books. All those trips to the public library really paid off! Thank you, Mom, for being my guardian angel. I wish you were here on earth with me to enjoy this journey. I never would have embarked on this adventure had you not taught me to chase my dreams fearlessly. Violeta and Lila, I love you both so much. You're a constant source of inspiration. Thank you to my critique group partners Annie, Christine, and Louise. You all are the best! Finally, thank you to my wonderful agent, Liza Fleissig; my amazing editor, Caroline Abbey; and the Random House team for your continued guidance and support.

# New friends. New adventures.
# Find a new series . . . just for you!

**ISADORA MOON**
For ballerina and fairy and vampire lovers

**MAGIC ON THE MAP**
For adventurers

**UNICORN ACADEMY**
For unicorn lovers

**PUPPY PIRATES**
For dog lovers

**PURRMAIDS**
For mermaid and cat lovers

**BALLPARK Mysteries**
For sports fans

**RHCB** rhcbooks.com